The Mice in Council

RETOLD AND ILLUSTRATED BY GRAHAM PERCY

The Child's World®

For Merle

Distributed in the United States of America by
The Child's World®
1980 Lookout Drive • Mankato, MN 56003-1705
800-599-READ • www.childsworld.com

ACKNOWLEDGMENTS
The Child's World®: Mary Berendes, Publishing Director
The Design Lab: Kathleen Petelinsek, Art Direction and Design;
Anna Petelinsek, Page Production

LIBRARY OF CONGRESS CATALOGING-IN-PUBLICATION DATA
Percy, Graham.
The mice in council / retold and illustrated by Graham Percy.
   p. cm. — (Aesop's fables)
 Summary: A family of mice meets to come up with ideas for dealing with
the cat that has been terrorizing, but when the seemingly perfect solution is
offered, they discover that thinking can be easier than doing.
  ISBN 978-1-60253-197-0 (lib. bound : alk. paper)
 [1. Fables. 2. Folklore.] I. Aesop. II. Title. III. Series.
 PZ8.2.P435Mic 2009
 398.2—dc22
 [E]   2009002045

Thinking up good ideas can be easier than acting on them.

There once was a family of mice who lived in a little country house. They should have been peaceful and happy, but they were not.

Do you know why?

A large cat made every day
terrible for the mice.

Each morning, the cat
crouched outside the window.
It watched the family eat
their breakfast. The little mice
trembled when they saw the
cat's shadow.

After breakfast, the older mice
dashed outside to gather food.
They scurried through weeds.
They hurried through leaves.
When they saw the cat's swishing
tail, they froze in fear.

After lunch, Mother Mouse
liked to work in her garden.
Soon two furry ears would
appear over the bushes. Mother
would scurry back into the
house. Sometimes she could not
get her weeding done.

In the afternoons, the two Mouse twins would play the piano. Soon their music could not even be heard! That is because the cat would sit outside, meowing loudly.

In the evenings, Father Mouse would close the curtains. Each time, the cat's yellow eye would appear at the window! Father would shrink back against the wall. He hoped the cat would not see him.

One day, Grandma and
Grandpa Mouse came to stay.
They enjoyed some quiet time
on the porch. Suddenly, a huge
paw appeared! Grandma and
Grandpa barely had time to
run inside.

"This is silly," said Grandpa Mouse. "Surely there must be something we can do to protect ourselves from the cat."

"I agree," said Father Mouse. He called a family meeting in the kitchen. Mother Mouse soon had an idea.

"If the cat had a bell around its neck," she suggested, "we would always know where it was. We would have plenty of time to get away."

"What a wonderful idea!" said Father Mouse. He gave his wife a hug.

Grandma Mouse was quiet. She thought for a moment. She shook her head.

"Which one of us will put the bell around the cat's neck?" she asked. "That is a very dangerous job."

The mice looked at one another.

"We cannot," said the youngest mice. "We are too small."

"We cannot," said the Mouse twins. "We are too scared."

"We cannot," said Mother and Father Mouse. "We are too slow."

"We cannot," said Grandma and Grandpa Mouse. "We are too old."

Father Mouse sighed.

"Thinking up good ideas," he said, "can be much easier than acting on them!"

AESOP

Aesop was a storyteller who lived more than 2,500 years ago. He lived so long ago, there isn't much information about him. Most people believe Aesop was a slave who lived in the area around the Mediterranean Sea—probably in or near the country of Greece.

Aesop's fables are known in almost every culture in the world, in almost every language. His fables are even *part* of some languages! Some common phrases come from Aesop's fables, such as "sour grapes" and "Don't count your chickens before they're hatched."

ABOUT FABLES

Fables are one of the oldest forms of stories. They are often short and funny, and have animals as the main characters. These animals act like people. Often, fables teach the reader a lesson. This is called a *moral*. A moral might teach right from wrong, or show how to act in good, kind ways. A moral might show what happens when someone makes a poor decision. Fables teach us how to live wisely.

ABOUT THE ILLUSTRATOR

Graham Percy was a famous illustrator of more than one hundred books. He was born and raised in New Zealand. He first studied art at the Elam School of Art in New Zealand and then moved to London, England, to study at the Royal College of Art.

Mr. Percy especially loved to draw animals, many types of which can be found in his books. He illustrated books on everything from mysteries to lullabies. He was even a designer for the animated film "Hugo the Hippo." Mr. Percy lived most of his life in London.